Margaret Wise Brown
Love Songs of the Little Bear

Love Song of the Little Bear

Green Song

Song of Wind & Rain

Snow Song

Pictures by Susan Jeffers

SCHOLASTIC INC.

New York Toronto London Auckland Sydney
Mexico City New Delhi Hong Kong Buenos Aires

For Alice Claudia Jeffers

ISBN 0-439-31702-9

Text copyright © 2001 by Roberta Brown Rauch.
Illustrations copyright © 2001 by Susan Jeffers.
All rights reserved.
Published by Scholastic Inc., 555 Broadway, New York, NY 10012,
by arrangement with Hyperion Books for Children, an imprint of Disney Children's Book Group, LLC.
SCHOLASTIC and associated logos are trademarks and/or registered trademarks of Scholastic Inc.

12 11 10 9 8 7 6 5 4 3 2 1   1 2 3 4 5 6/0

Printed in Mexico   49

First Scholastic printing, September 2001

Love Song of the Little Bear

By the clear waters
One morning in May
A little bear was singing
In words that seemed to say

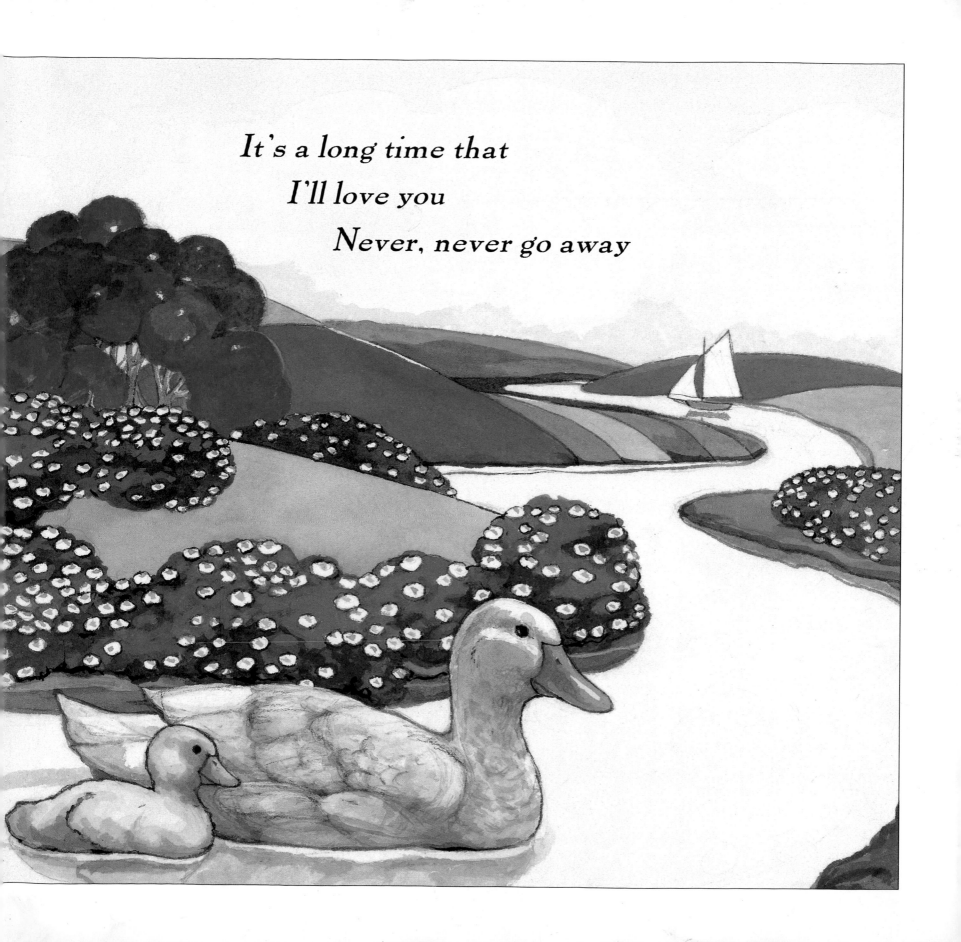

It's a long time that
I'll love you
Never, never go away

It's a long time that I'll love you

And if I seem to stray

It's only that I'm watching
The flowers bloom in May.

Float little glass bottles
On waters green and gray

It's only you I'm loving
On this bright green day.

Float little bottles

With messages that say

It's a long time that I'll love you

Never, never go away.

That is the love song
Of the little bear today

That is my little love song
And all I have to say.

Green Song

I'll sing a green song
*S*ing me your green song

A song of the deep green tangled deep
Where little prickly spiders creep

Deep in their long-stemmed world.

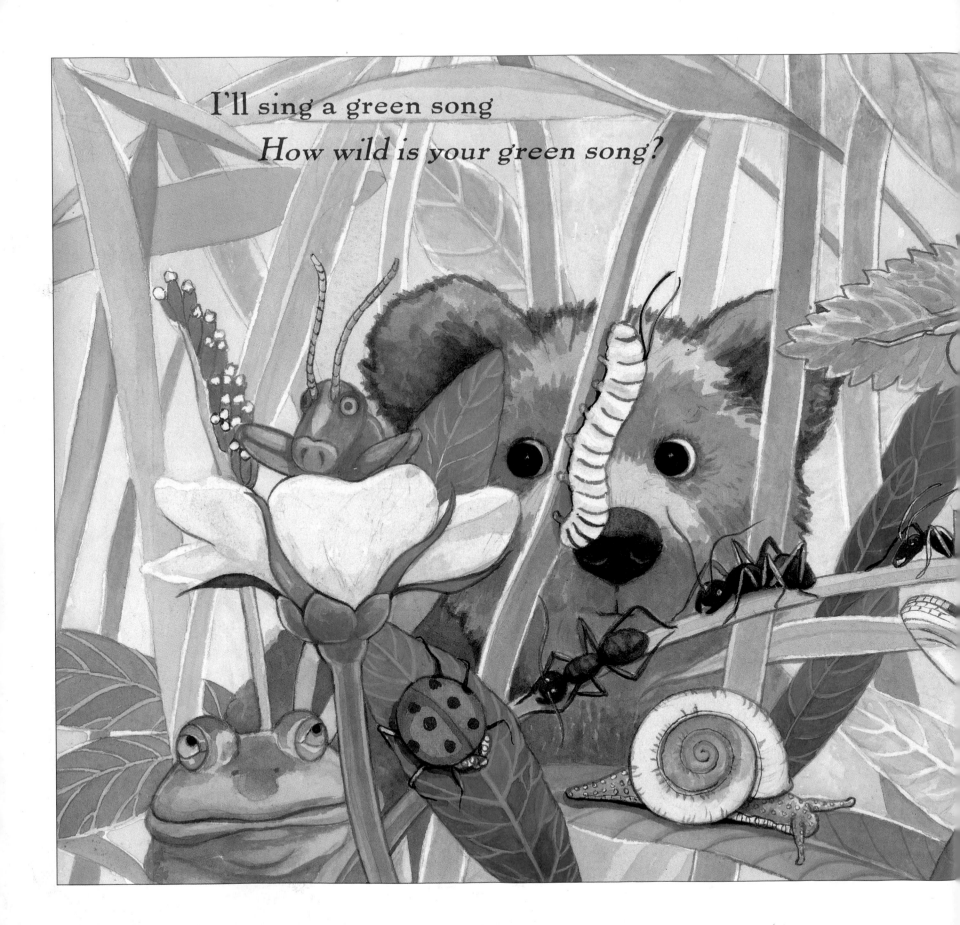

I'll sing a green song

How wild is your green song?

Wild as a world where little things creep
In their green grass forests deep
Deep in their long-stemmed world.

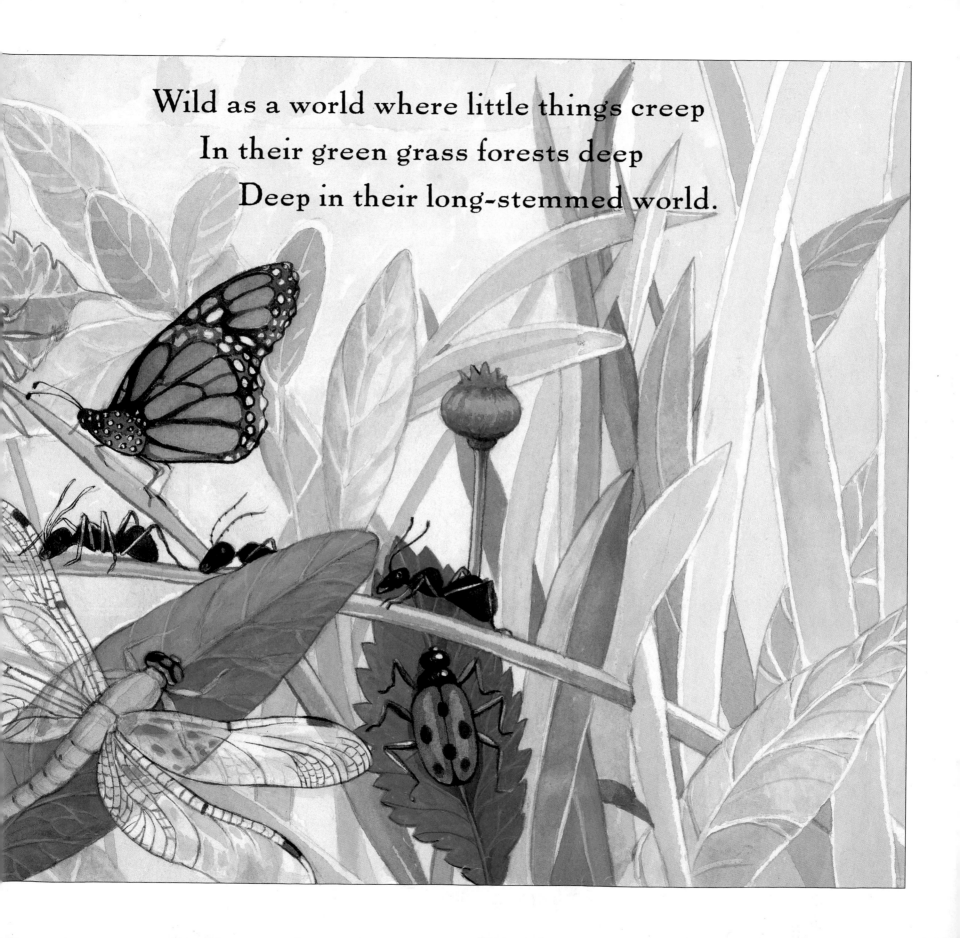

I'll sing a green song

Sing me your green song

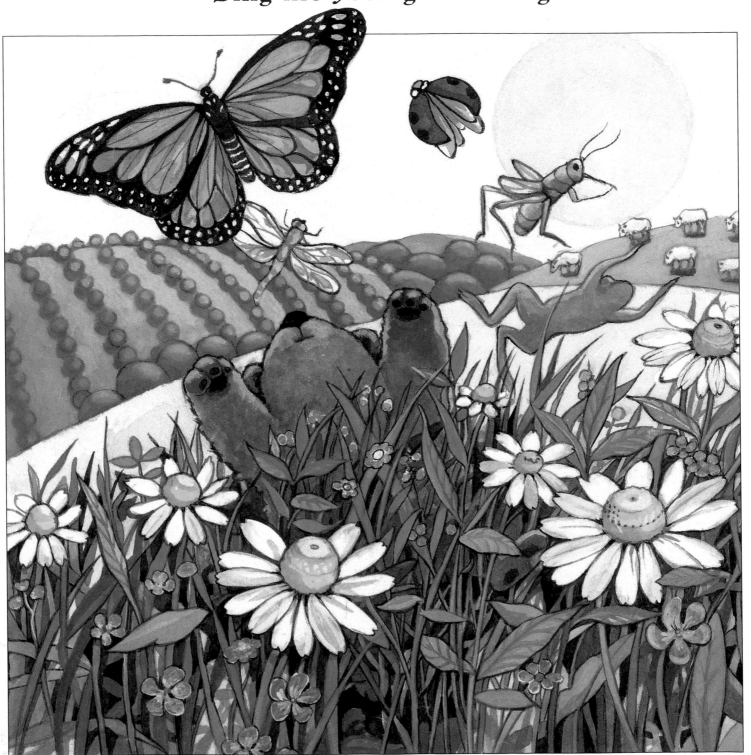

A song of the deep green tangled deep
Where the little bugs are all asleep

Deep in their long-stemmed world.

Song of Wind & Rain

There was once a brave little bear
Who flew through the wind and the rain

And he heard their songs again and again,
The songs that are sung to a little bear.

I am the rain

the rain

the rain

I get you wet,

Little Bear.

I am the wind
the wind
the wind

I blow the rain
And I blow you,
Little Bear

Rain and wind
Wind and rain

Sing to us all,
my Little Bear.

Snow Song

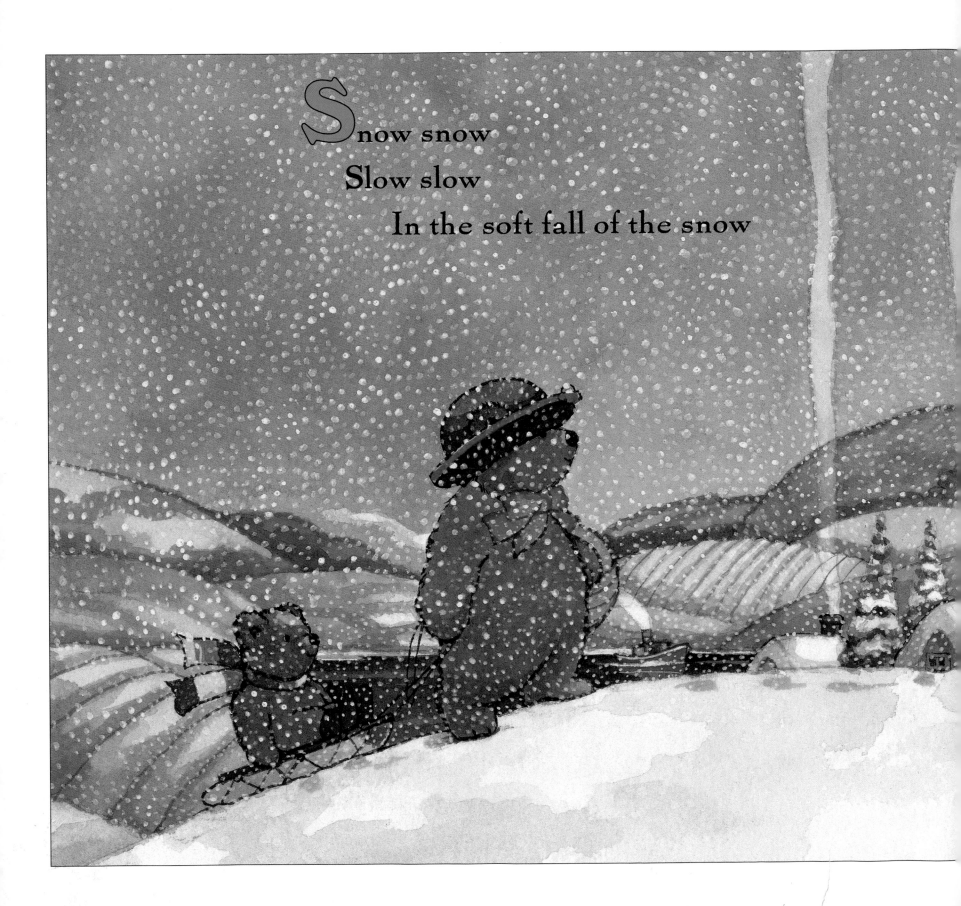

Snow snow
Slow slow
In the soft fall of the snow

The little boats go.

The bell buoys ring
And the whistles blow

While the boats go slowly
Over the river through the snow.

Slow

Slow

In the soft fall of the snow
The little bears go.

They walk in wonder
Under the frosted trees of fairyland
Into the falling snow

To the lighted doors
That open
Into home.

Artist's Note

"Snow snow
   Slow slow
      In the soft fall of the snow . . ."

In reading those words, I was a child again, walking with my mother. Together with my sister, we went on Spring Walks, Summer Walks, Fall Walks, and, best of all, After the Ice Storm Walks. Whatever the season, my mother had a gift for slowing down time. We stopped and looked at everything—scarlet leaves, heart-shaped stones, blue roadside glass. It was wordless poetry.

Margaret Wise Brown also slows down the speeding world to the pace of a child's walk. To truly appreciate what her poetry says about the enduring love and the profound beauty of the everyday, readers must go at her pace, the pace of childhood.

I was honored to be invited to illustrate a group of Margaret Wise Brown's unpublished poems. In researching her poetry, I learned that she often wrote many versions of a single poem. She also left many lovely fragments of poetry that reminded me of haiku in their simplicity. How was I to choose between versions, to be certain a fragment was finished? It was in reading the title poem, "Love Song of the Little Bear," that I could envision a book, one in which a young character, a family, and a setting could express the connection between my experience as a child and the work of Margaret Wise Brown. I hope she would approve of my choices.

—S.J.